W9-AUS-330

Paulette Bogan

VIRGIL & OWEN Stick Together

BLOOMSBURY
NEW YORK LONDON OXFORD NEW DELHI SYDNEY

Copyright © 2016 by Paulette Bogan
All rights reserved. No part of this book may be reproduced or transmitted in any form or by any means,
electronic or mechanical, including photocopying, recording, or by any information storage and retrieval
system, without permission in writing from the publisher.

First published in the United States of America in January 2016
by Bloomsbury Children's Books
www.bloomsbury.com

Bloomsbury is a registered trademark of Bloomsbury Publishing Plc

For information about permission to reproduce selections from this book, write to
Permissions, Bloomsbury Children's Books, 1385 Broadway, New York, New York 10018
Bloomsbury books may be purchased for business or promotional use. For information on bulk purchases
please contact Macmillan Corporate and Premium Sales Department at specialmarkets@macmillan.com

Library of Congress Cataloging-in-Publication Data
Bogan, Paulette, author, illustrator.
Virgil & Owen stick together / by Paulette Bogan.
      pages   cm
Summary: Owen the polar bear and Virgil the penguin both love going to school . . . just in different ways. Eager
Virgil likes to learn as much as he can, as quickly as possible. Owen likes to savor each moment as he counts and
writes and tells stories. So when Virgil rushes Owen a bit too much one day, their friendship is suddenly on thin
ice. Can Virgil exercise some patience and appreciate his friend's point of view?
ISBN 978-1-61963-373-5 (hardcover) • ISBN 978-1-61963-931-7 (e-book) • ISBN 978-1-61963-932-4 (e-PDF)
[1. Friendship—Fiction. 2. Patience—Fiction. 3. Penguins—Fiction. 4. Polar bear—Fiction. 5. Bears—Fiction.]
I. Title. II. Title: Virgil and Owen stick together.
PZ7.B6357835Vl 2016   [E]—dc23   2015021236

Art created with Sakura Micron pens (waterproof) and Winsor Newton Water Colour and Gouache,
on Arches cold press watercolor paper
Typeset in Bodoni Egyptian
Book design by Amanda Bartlett

Printed in China by Leo Paper Products, Heshan, Guangdong
1 3 5 7 9 10 8 6 4 2

All papers used by Bloomsbury Publishing, Inc., are natural, recyclable products
made from wood grown in well-managed forests. The manufacturing processes
conform to the environmental regulations of the country of origin.

To making friends with your polar opposite!

And thank you, Mary Kate Castellani,
Donna Mark, and Amanda Bartlett

Virgil and Owen walked to school together.

"Let's move it," said Virgil. "We'll be late."

Owen liked math.

"One . . . two . . . three . . ."

"Four, five, *SIX*," said Virgil.

"Easy peasy, my friend."

Owen liked writing his letters.

"**E**, **N**. *Owen*," said Virgil.

"That was fun."

Owen liked story time.
"And then . . . ," said Owen.

"It was the whale, Owen," said Virgil.
"The whale did it! **THE END!**"

"Grrr . . ."

Owen loved lunch.
"Yum, seaweed sandwiches."

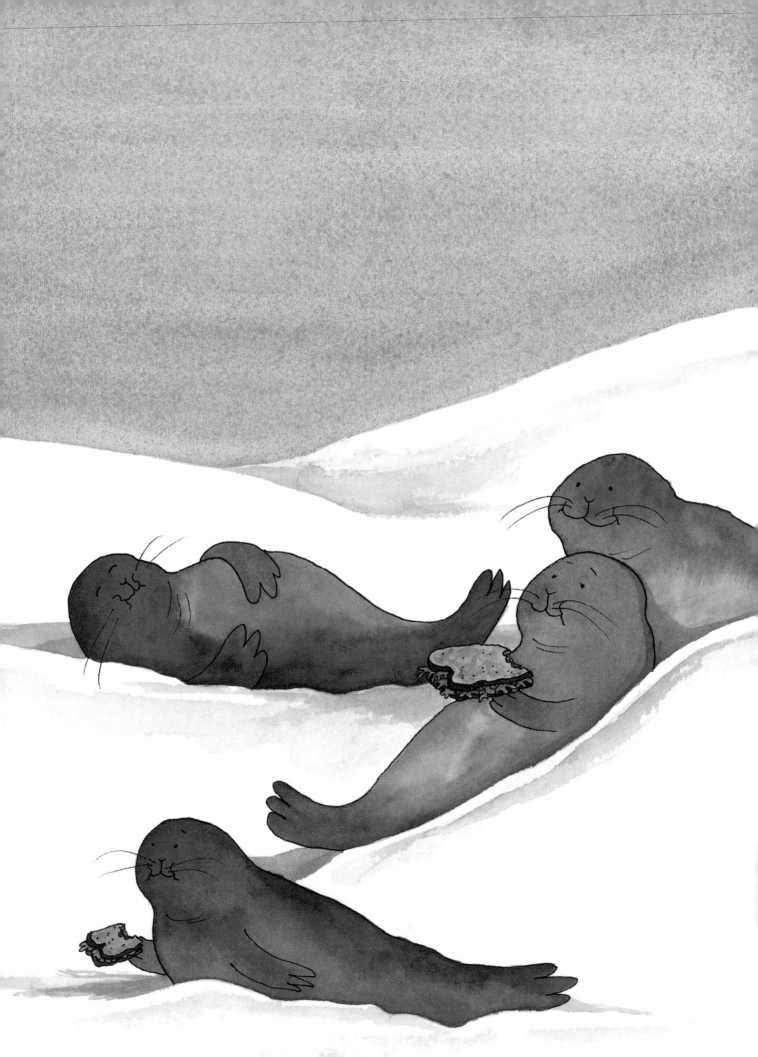

"Are you going to eat that?" asked Virgil.
"Lunch is **OVER!** *Hurry UP!*"

RROOAARRR

"I don't want to hurry up."

Um . . . no rush."

"Owen . . . I'm sorry."

Owen and Virgil walked home
together . . . *really* slowly.

"Sorry I roared at you, Virgil,"
said Owen.

"We will just take our time," said Virgil.
"No rush at all. All the time in the world.
Yep, nice and slow."